THE BEE'S SNEEZE

ELLIS NADLER

Simon & Schuster Books for Young Readers
Published by Simon & Schuster
New York London Toronto
Sydney Tokyo Singapore

SIMON & SCHUSTER BOOKS FOR YOUNG READERS
Simon & Schuster Building, Rockefeller Center
1230 Avenue of the Americas, New York, New York   10020
Copyright © 1993 by Ellis Nadler
All rights reserved including the right of reproduction
in whole or in part in any form.
Originally published in Great Britain in 1993
by David Bennett Books Ltd.
SIMON & SCHUSTER BOOKS FOR YOUNG READERS
is a trademark of Simon & Schuster.
Manufactured in Singapore
10 9 8 7 6 5 4 3 2 1

Library of Congress Cataloging-in-Publication Data

Nadler, Ellis.
    The bee's sneeze / Ellis Nadler.
      p.cm.
    Summary: A bee's sneeze saves the lives of several animals
in this cumulative, rhyming story.
    [1. Animals—Fiction.   2. Stories in rhyme.] I. Title.
PZ8.3.N9975Be   1993
[E]—dc20
ISBN: 0–671–86575–7

For Samuel

A bumblebee said, with a wheeze,
"I think I am going to sneeze."

A spider appeared from thin air
And swallowed the bee then and there.

A greedy frog's mouth opened wide,
As he stuffed that fat spider inside.

A duck waddled down from the hill
And scooped up the frog in his bill.

A raccoon reached down from the trees
And gobbled the duck with some cheese.

The raccoon fell down through the air,
Straight into the mouth of a bear.

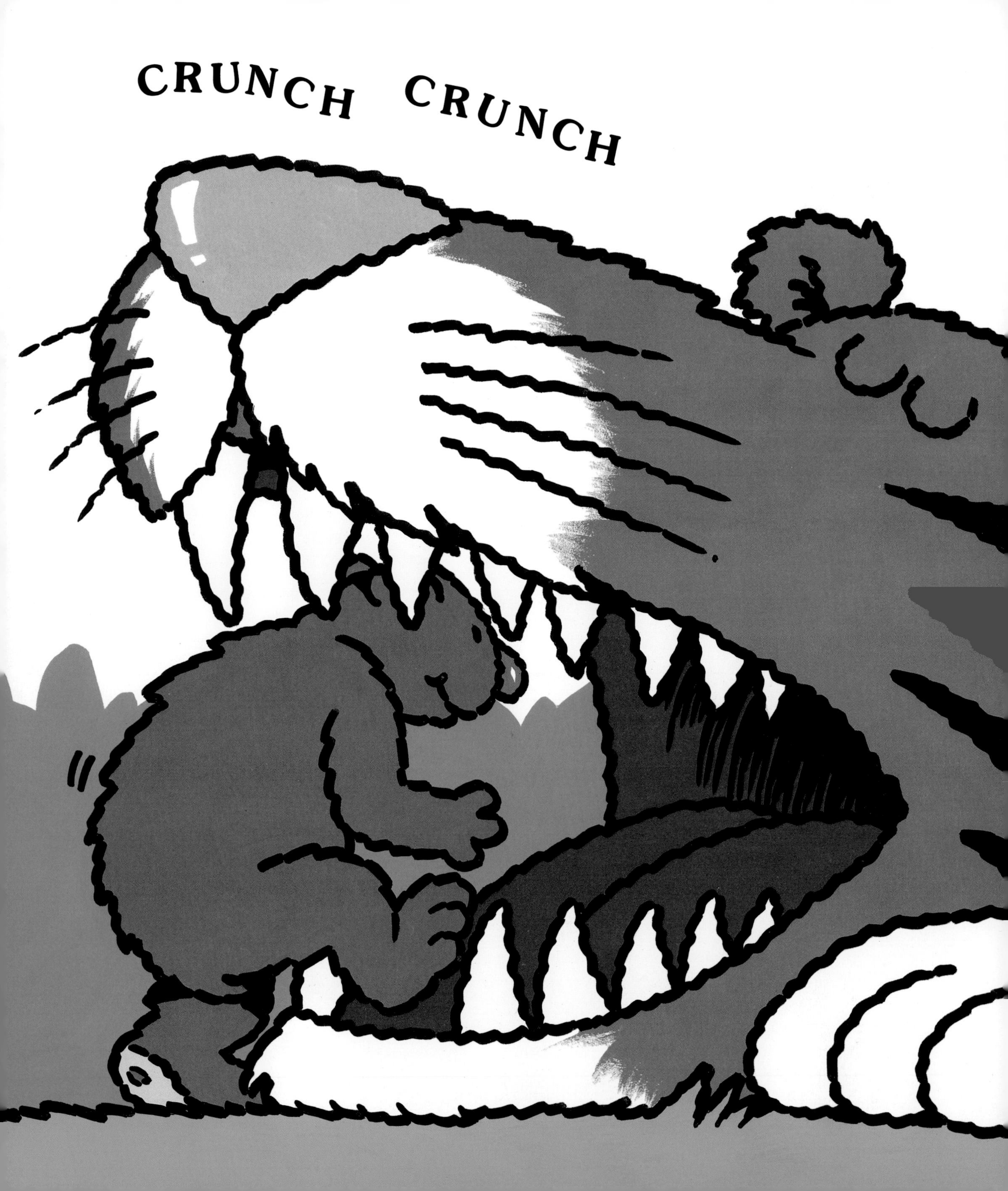
CRUNCH CRUNCH

A tiger was going to roar,
When the bear padded in to explore.

The tiger was in for a shock,
Snapped up in the jaws of a croc.

A whale swam up from below
And swallowed the croc in one go.

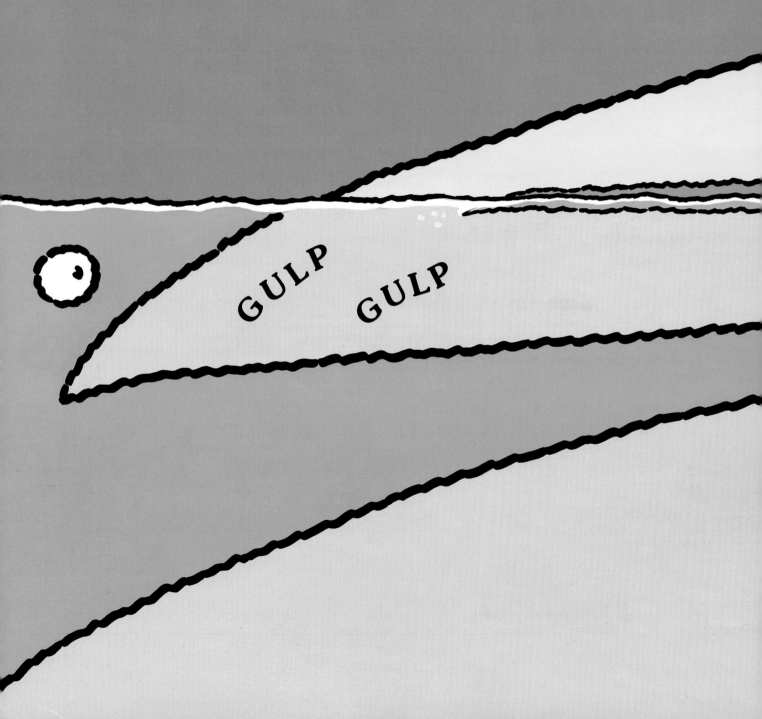

But deep down inside that huge whale,
The bee had turned terribly pale.
A tremble went right through his knees,
And he let out an almighty . . .

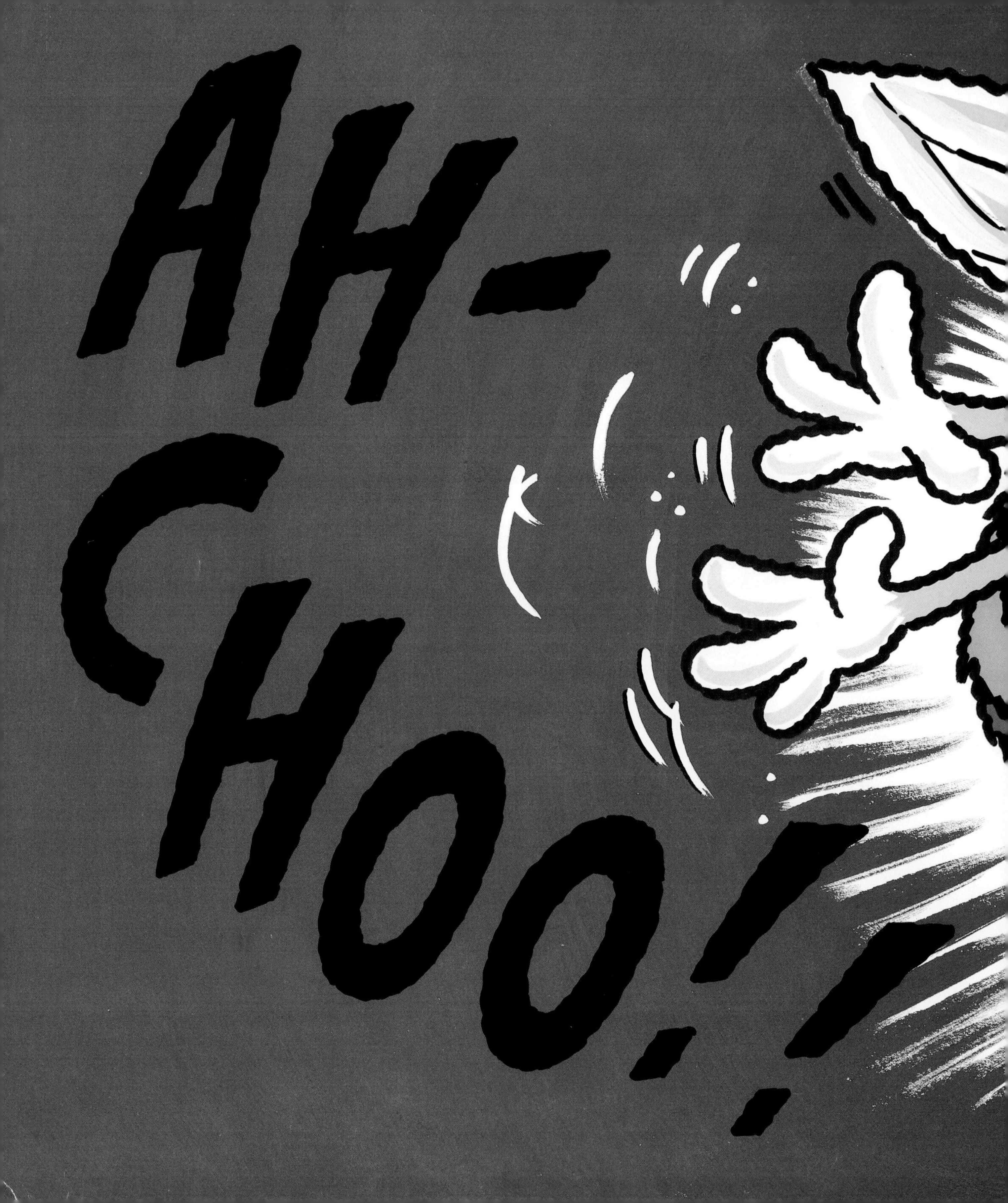
AH-CHOO!!

The spider awoke . . .

which made the frog choke . . .

the frog kicked the duck . . .

the raccoon ran amok . . .

the bear clutched his tum . . .

the tiger went numb . . .

the croc did a flip . . .

the whale bit his lip . . .

and let out a mighty . . .

The animals all tumbled out
And started to sing and to shout.

As the whale swam back out to sea,
The animals cried, "Bless you, Bee!"